C0-AFH-764

Night in the Gardens
J.H. Low

mc Marshall Cavendish
Children

Mum tucked Mei into bed and kissed her goodnight.
She switched off the lights and whispered, “Sleep tight!”
Alone in her room, Mei tossed and turned.
Try as she might, she could not sleep.
Not even when she tried counting sheep.

Then she heard a gentle whisper.
"Hello Mei, are you awake?
Shall we take a little break?"

Mei peeked out from under her covers.
It was Adventurous Andy the bear!
"Well," he said, "shall we enjoy the cool night air?"

Adventurous Andy held Mei by the hand.
He led her out the window feeling grand!
Then he let out a whistle long into the night.
Oh, what fun they'll have with the stars shining bright!

Adventurous Andy's call was heard
by a giant kingfisher that appeared.
It was the largest Mei had ever seen!
The beautiful bird was brown, blue and green.

Adventurous Andy looked at Mei
with a twinkle in his eye.
"What do you think, Mei?
Are you ready to fly?"

Mei nodded excitedly and off they went.
Higher and higher they ascended into the sky.
Faster and faster they sped by.

Mei closed her eyes and held her breath.
She wondered when they would come to a rest.

Mustering her courage, she opened her eyes.
Soon she was taking it all in her stride.

Looking around her, Mei was amazed.
What she saw made her a little dazed.
The night was not at all what she had thought.
It was not dark nor was it scary.
In fact, it was quite the contrary.

The night was bright with glistening lights.
Cars, buses and trucks with shining headlights.
There were also buildings, bridges
and a huge turning wheel with fairy lights.
"The Singapore Flyer!" Mei exclaimed.

"1, 2, 3…" Mei counted the lights merrily, "4, 5, 6…"
All of a sudden, twinkling lights
of a thousand colours surrounded Mei.
"Where are we? What's going on?" she cried.

“It’s the Supertrees!” chuckled Adventurous Andy.

“Oooh! We are at Gardens by the Bay!” gasped Mei.

Gardens by the Bay was a fairy tale land at night.
All aglow with enchanted lights.
Oh, what a magnificent sight.

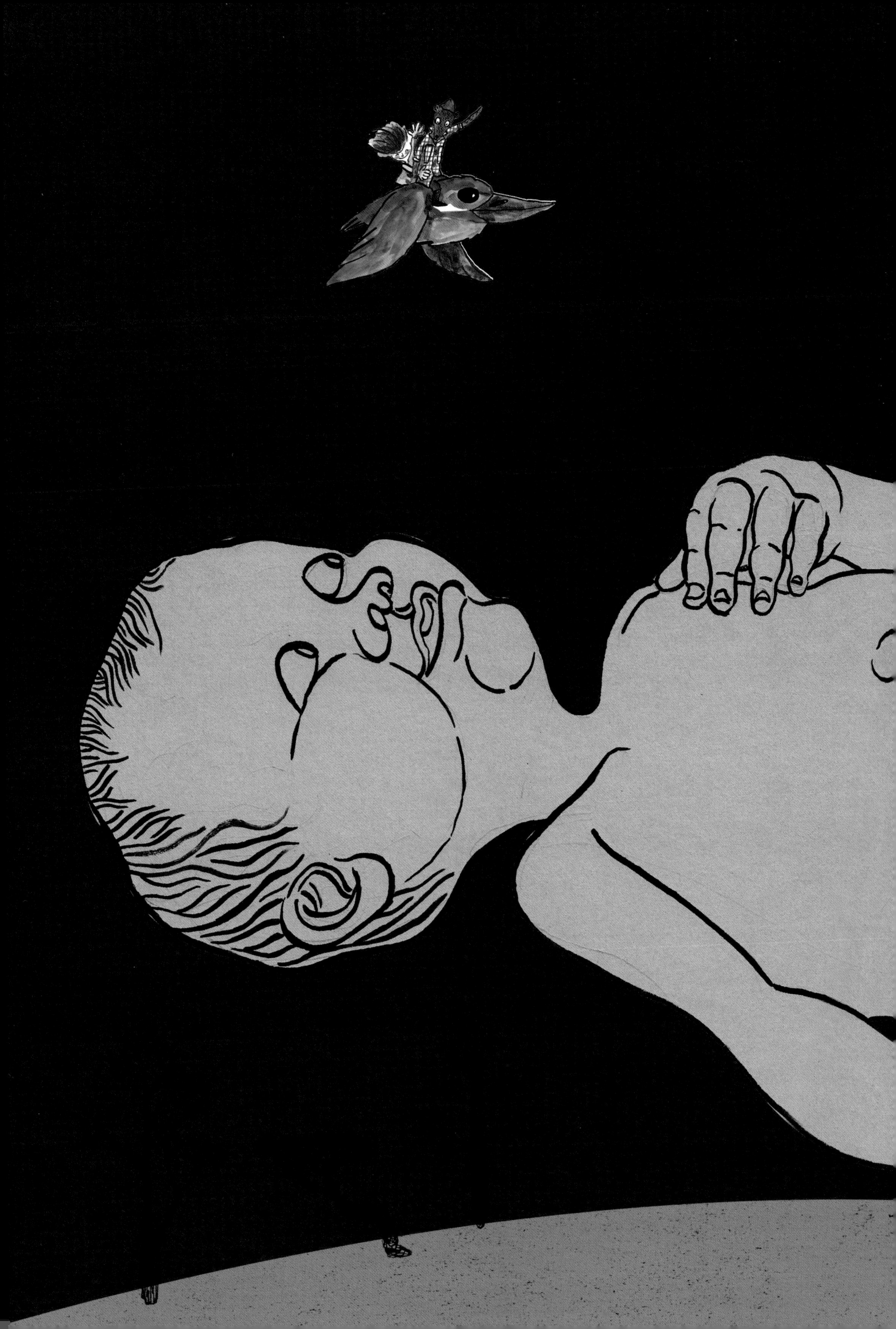

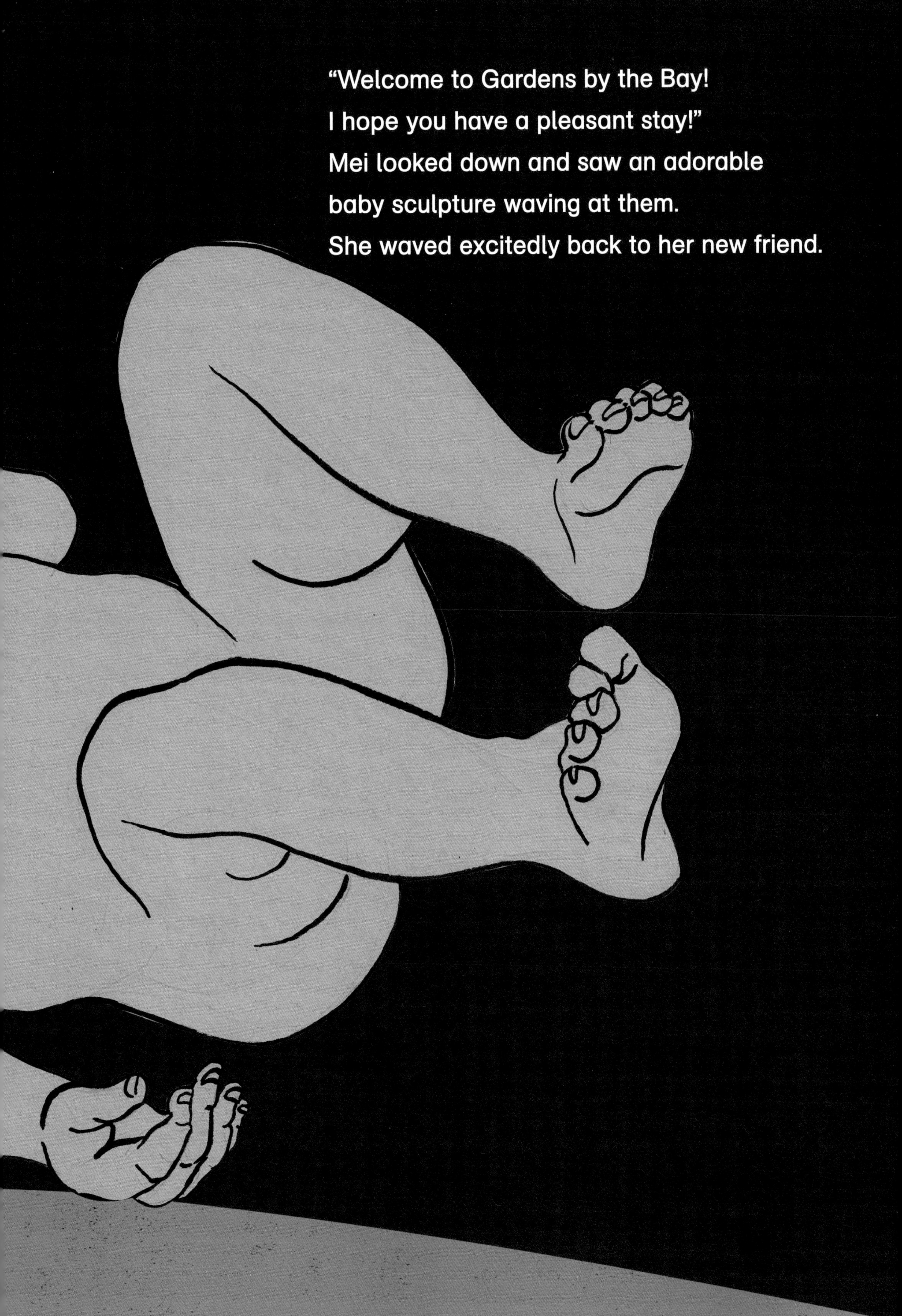

"Welcome to Gardens by the Bay!
I hope you have a pleasant stay!"
Mei looked down and saw an adorable
baby sculpture waving at them.
She waved excitedly back to her new friend.

Into the mystical Cloud Forest the kingfisher flew,
giving Mei and Adventurous Andy a glorious bird's eye view!
They stood by the majestic waterfall,
taking in the beauty of the place at nightfall.

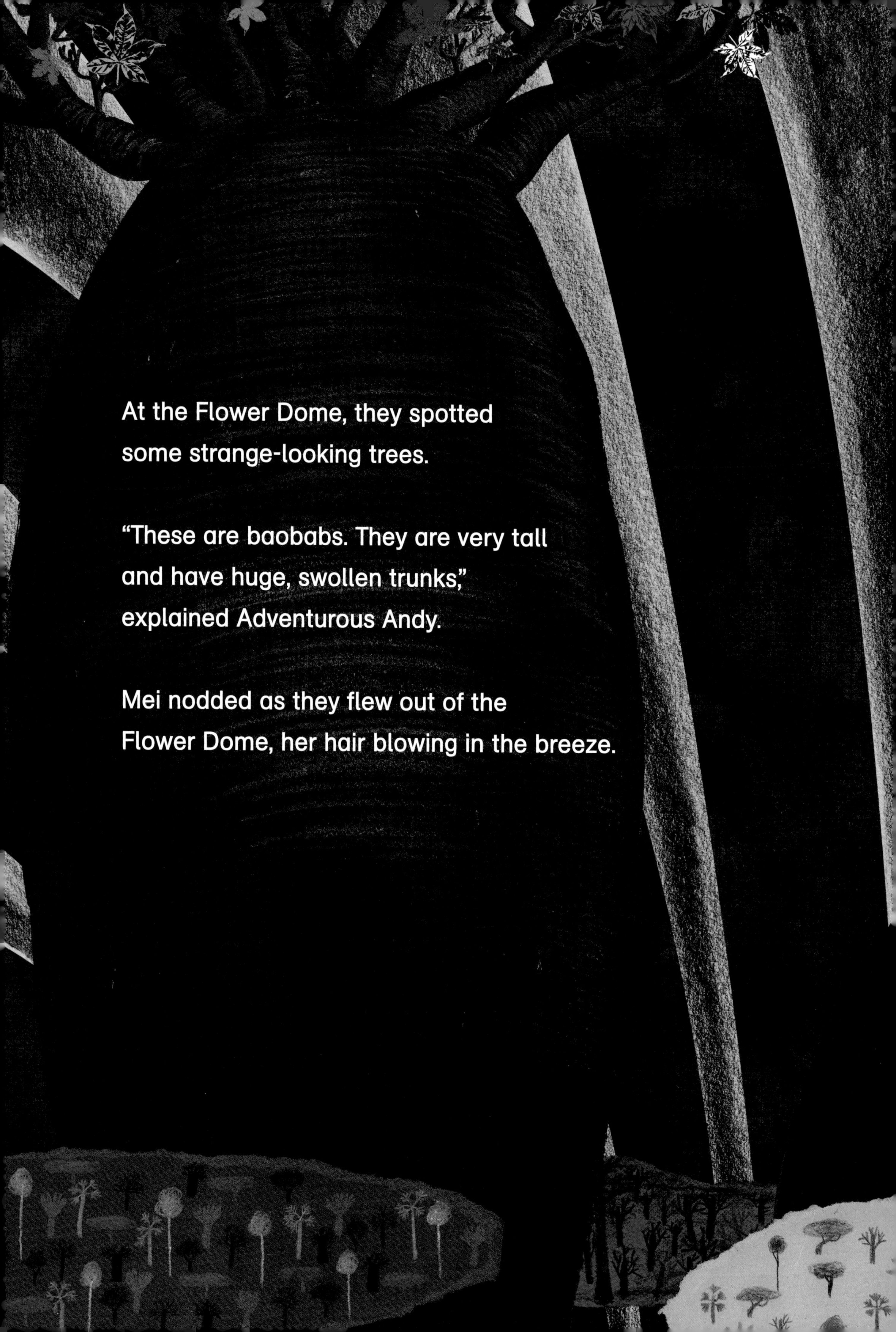

At the Flower Dome, they spotted some strange-looking trees.

“These are baobabs. They are very tall and have huge, swollen trunks,” explained Adventurous Andy.

Mei nodded as they flew out of the Flower Dome, her hair blowing in the breeze.

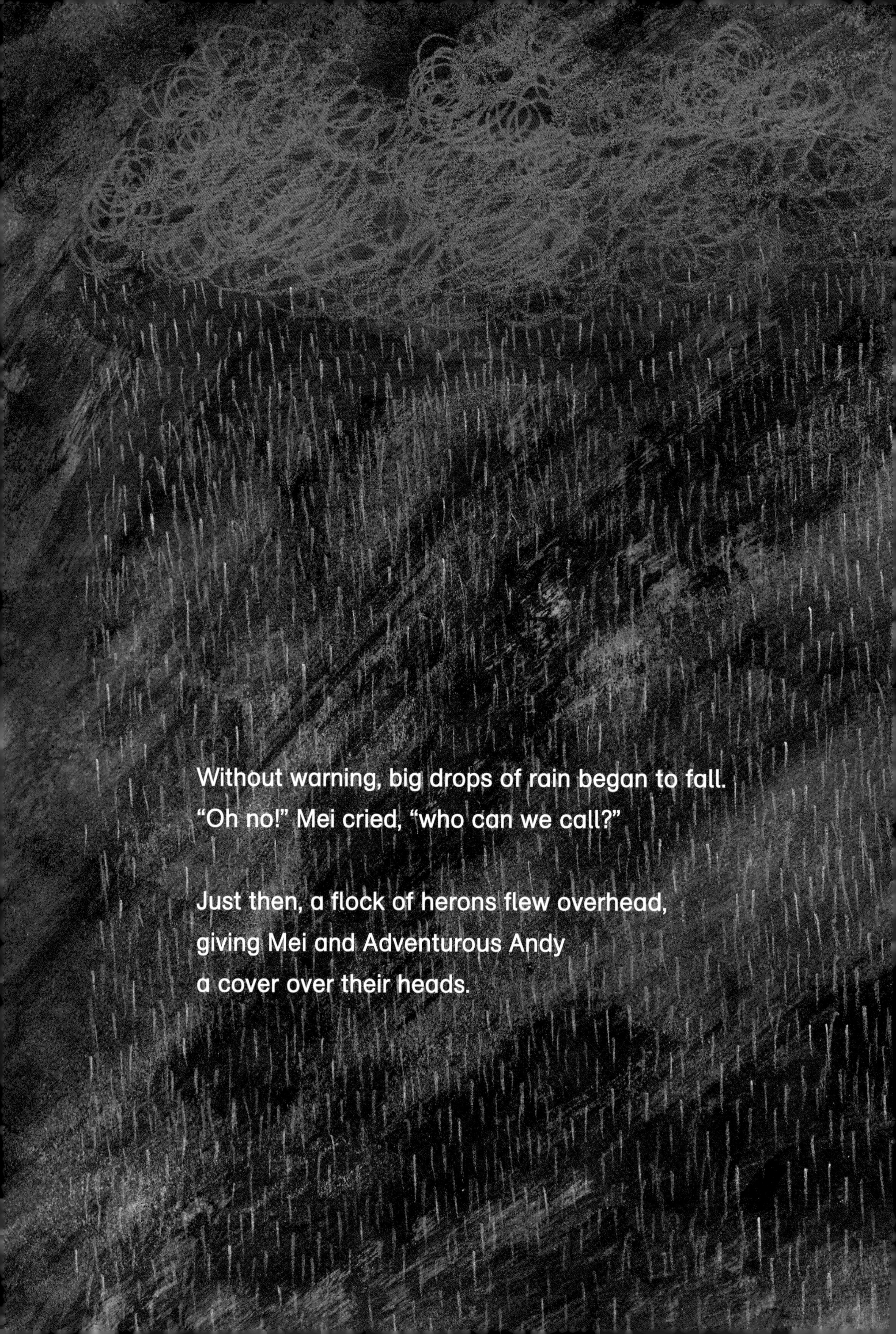

Without warning, big drops of rain began to fall.
“Oh no!” Mei cried, “who can we call?”

Just then, a flock of herons flew overhead,
giving Mei and Adventurous Andy
a cover over their heads.

The rain soon tapered off
and the stars twinkled brightly once again.

"I'm hungry," Mei said as her tummy rumbled.

"I know just the place to go," smiled Adventurous Andy.
"Let's head to Satay by the Bay!"

Surprise, surprise! When they got there,
waiting for them was Wise Wee the bear!
"Welcome!" he smiled, "I've prepared supper to share!"

satay
by the bay

He brought them a big plate of satay.
A dish of grilled skewered meat
with a spicy peanut dip.
Mei tried her best not to let the sauce drip.

Next, he prepared *ice kacang*.
A treat of shaved ice with coloured syrup.
In it were red beans, sweetcorn kernels
and cubes of agar-agar jelly.
When she finished eating,
Mei licked her lips
and rubbed her little belly.

Soon, it was time for Mei to head home.
She gave Wise Wee a big hug
and a peck on the cheek.
"Thank you Wise Wee for the lovely treat.
Tonight has been very sweet!"

Then off on the giant kingfisher's back they sped.
Oh, what an eventful night they had!

Back home, Mei yawned as Adventurous Andy tucked her into bed.
Memories of their adventure were still fresh in her head.
She smiled as he waved goodbye and she was alone once more.
Mei was no longer afraid as she was before.
She now knew that the night was not dark nor scary after all.

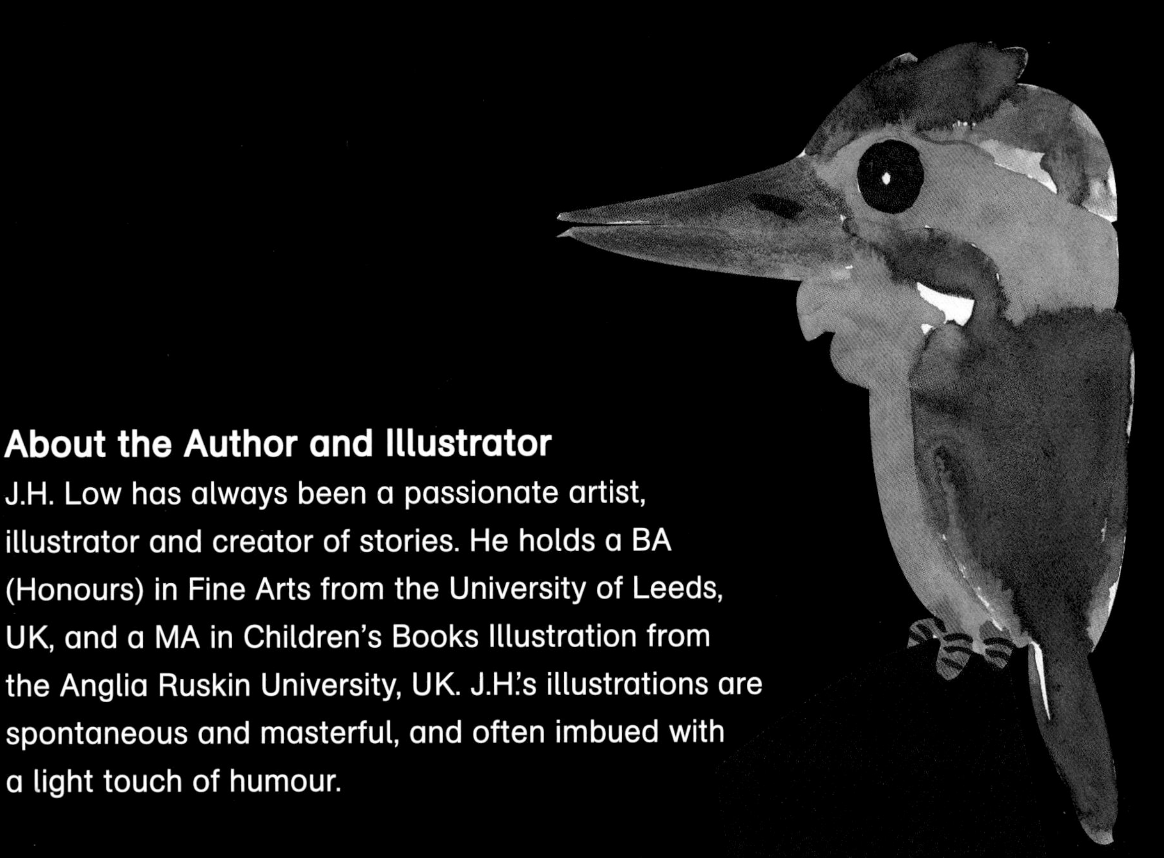

About the Author and Illustrator

J.H. Low has always been a passionate artist, illustrator and creator of stories. He holds a BA (Honours) in Fine Arts from the University of Leeds, UK, and a MA in Children's Books Illustration from the Anglia Ruskin University, UK. J.H.'s illustrations are spontaneous and masterful, and often imbued with a light touch of humour.

In 2009, he received Honourable Mention for the prestigious Macmillan Prize for his book, *There Is Nothing Buried Here*. The book is now part of a five-book series, Four Tooth and Friends, which has been published in English and Chinese. Two other titles in the series, *The Hyena and the Monster* and *A Thief in the Night*, won the Samsung KidsTime Author's Award 2016, Grand Prize and Second Prize respectively.

J.H. is also the illustrator of *Dragon's Egg* by award-winning author, Carolyn Goodwin. *Night in the Gardens* is the second title in a series by J.H. on Singapore's attractions. The first title, *Lost in the Gardens*, was a finalist in the Singapore Book Awards 2016 for Best Children's Title.

Published by Marshall Cavendish Children
An imprint of Marshall Cavendish International

Other Marshall Cavendish Offices:
Marshall Cavendish Corporation, 800 Westchester Ave, Suite N-641, Rye Brook, NY 10573, USA • Marshall Cavendish International (Thailand) Co Ltd, 253 Asoke, 16th Floor, Sukhumvit 21 Road, Klongtoey Nua, Wattana, Bangkok 10110, Thailand • Marshall Cavendish (Malaysia) Sdn Bhd, Times Subang, Lot 46, Subang Hi-Tech Industrial Park, Batu Tiga, 40000 Shah Alam, Selangor Darul Ehsan, Malaysia

National Library Board, Singapore Cataloguing-in-Publication Data

Name(s): Low, Joo Hong.
Title: Night in the gardens / J. H. Low.
Description: Singapore : Marshall Cavendish Children, [2016]
Identifier(s): OCN 951229005 | ISBN 978-981-47-5142-1 (hardcover)
Subject(s): LCSH: Night--Juvenile fiction. | Fear of the dark--Juvenile fiction.
Classification: DDC 428.6--dc23

Printed in Singapore